PROSE.

POEMS.

a novel.

ISBN 10: 0-9817481-2-0
ISBN 13: 978-0-9817481-2-2

Library of Congress Control Number: 2009907267

Drawings "black bear," "psilocybin," "snake hair, face," "deer head," "mosquitos," and "bullet wound" © 2009, by Christy Call. Used by permission of the artist. For information, go to www.christycall.com.

Orange Alert Press
PO Box 3897
St. Charles, IL 60174

www.orangealert.net

PROSE.

POEMS.

a novel.

JAMIE IREDELL

Acknowledgements

I'm grateful to the editors of the following magazines, where many parts of this book first appeared, sometimes in different form:

3:AM, The Angler, Copper Nickel, The Corduroy Mtn, Dogzplot, elimae, Hotel St. George, Keyhole, Lamination Colony, The Lifted Brow, Mud Luscious, NANO Fiction, Oranges and Sardines, Pank, Storyscape, THE2NDHAND, Thieves Jargon, Titular Journal, Wigleaf, and *Willows Wept Review*

Portions of this book were published as the chapbooks *Before I Moved to Nevada* (Publishing Genius Press), *When I Moved to Nevada* (The Greying Ghost Press), and *Atlanta* (Paper Hero Press). Many thanks to Adam Robinson, Carl Annarummo, and Barry Graham—the editors of these presses—for publishing my work.

Many thanks to those who read incarnations of this manuscript and, in some cases, specific pieces within it: Sara Bartlett, Christopher Bundy, Blake Butler, Laura Carter, Mike Dockins, Man Martin, and Laura McCullough.

Thanks to Jason Behrends at Orange Alert Press for publishing this book! And thanks so much to Christy Call, whose art helps make this book an art object in itself.

Thanks to Gailmarie Pahmeier, who gave me her copy of Denis Johnson's *Jesus' Son*, and to Stuart Dybek, for *The Coast of Chicago*.

Thanks to the Iredells (Bryan, Dad, Meghann, Mom, and Julie), and Mike Dockins, who is a goon, and who—as Dean Young says of Tony Hoagland—is my brother.

Of course: Sarah Babcock.

Contents

FOR JASON, MY BROTHER, WHO LOVED IT ALL
AND FOR JULES

"There are two kinds of people in this world, my friend. Those with loaded guns, and those who dig."

—Clint Eastwood

California cameras eyeball a Western landscape. The distant mesas are enormous tables. A gangly actor—and by this I mean that under the make-up, in real life, he is fat, short, and pimple-faced—saunters into the saloon, swinging his dusty be-pistoled leg, the bar backgrounded, miles away. The patrons hush—even the piano sitter, who adorns an unplaying piano, for the Stephen Foster will later be dubbed in. Cut. I'll smoke this cigar. Give me a damsel. Someone guzzle a beer. This should be Atlanta, ca. 2006. Towers tower for a skyline. Now this is a Western. The script begins: A whiskered goon at a notepad. Tumbleweeds. Crickets.

Book I:

Before I Moved to Nevada

"Between my finger and my thumb
The squat pen rests; as snug as a gun."

—from "Digging" by Seamus Heaney

The bear in the neighbors' kitchen was a black bear. Perhaps a brown cabin kitchen bear amongst these snowy mountains. The bear in the neighbors' kitchen pushed in the kitchen door. The bear in the neighbors' kitchen seemed to know that no one lived there. The bear in the neighbors' kitchen rooted through the drawers. The bear in the neighbors' kitchen in the open refrigerator's light. The bear in the neighbors' kitchen found the oat and cornmeal. The bear in the neighbors' kitchen wore butter on its face. The bear in the neighbors' kitchen left a stinky gift on the deck. The bear in the neighbors' kitchen trundled down the driveway. I could've called the neighbor about the bear in their kitchen. The neighbors have kitchens in houses—not mountain cabins—where they live year-round, where there is no snow, and no bears. I could've chased away the bear in the neighbors' kitchen. I could've been the bear in the neighbors' kitchen. I could've trapped the kitchen bear for the neighbors. My black kitchen hair. My bear.

We met at the football field, and the sun was how it gets in California: bright and hot. To smoke a joint, Randy, me, and this guy Ike— "like the soul singer, you know"—shuffled off for a Nissan glinting in the parking lot. Afterwards we lazed back into the high school smelling like Mexico and wishing Mexico was where we were. Ike would end up dumping my sister, and I would want to pummel him like any guy named Ike deserves to be pummeled. Eventually, though, I forgot about it. Until now.

The cops said, "Step out of the car." We had parked at the Slough, this place that could've been prehistoric, for its waters and fogged-in eucalypti, pelicans dive-bombing for sardines, otters smacking up abalone on their little bellies. We seesawed the dock and the waves rocked out below the sky and our descent into the water was so slow that millennia lived by and our shoes wouldn't even get soaked. They said we couldn't drive home. Later, Ike felt a joint tucked into a shirt pocket, unfound during the pat-down, and one end of it bound for the Nissan's cigarette lighter. Beyond the trees the power plant glowed red, and made the fog do the same. I knew in the future—within the hour—I'd drive toward the light, and past it.

At Zmudowski State Beach the waves crested up and we paddled them in. The football shuttled from our fingertips. Driving away, Ben's foot was heavy as a locomotive—which was how we steamed through the artichoke fields, weaving around corners, disregarding the softness of our flesh jiggling in the truck cab. When we launched from the berm into the green thistles, and jostled and blinked, we'd landed safely, the engine still ticking. We floored out of the crop, mud spitting behind us. That night the streets slicked with the light reflected in rainwater. We guzzled Zimas at a condo in Salinas. Leaving, in the same pickup, Ben again gave it too much gas. His father raced the track in Watsonville, and Ben sold parts at Pettigrew and Folletta after school, and this experience gave him the impression of control. We 360ed, came out facing the way we'd started. Ben had a moustache at fourteen. We called him "Dover," and also "Chewy," for all the hair. In his Xmas card he's smiling, bald, with his wife and four girls, three of them triplets.

The fog lilts in like a cat—perhaps a bear—as it stalks the coast and harbor, pounces artichoke fields, sinks its claws into the browned hillsides, and the fog's teeth settles in bones like a cold stalk of broccoli, like the earth in which it grows, sunless black, the recesses of space, above the moon, past the atmosphere, far beyond this Pacific cloud cover, and below water the sharks missile-cruise the forested kelp for seals, for the succulent fat beneath their skin, and between the shark jaws, in place of teeth, flex rusty bear traps, and if the sharks could, and you could maneuver it, they would let you gnaw yourself free and swim a strawberry trail to shore for the lettuce ripening in the valley, and the strawberries reddening in the hills, because fog is also good for this.

The party was in Simonville, an apt name, considering someone named Simon once herded cattle over the land. Now exactly eight trailers gathered make for a total of thirty-two-and-a-half villagers. Randy gazed starward, into the sky's kaleidoscope. A burn barrel burned our backs. "Dee Hernandez" and "cops" drifted in from a pair of lips. Me and Dee collided daily on a football field. The steroids—and his ridiculous first name—made him grunt and punch and scream at his teammates. He was a cop target for the coke he pinched into tiny sacks. Randy and me leapt over the fence where my back met a mass of stinging nettle. Dee wasn't even at that party. I kicked down the fence instead of clambering back over. We continued drinking Crazy Horse.

The sign—Pedestrian Xing—beamed out the Pontiac's window, the 4 x 4 that once held it in the Earth a slash across the back seat's vinyl. The night extinguished the lights in the fog. Dave was our left guard, though he could've been a running back, for his svelte size and his speed. Dave was also the first guy to have given my sister a smack on the lips. When the headlights of another car beamed down Tustin Road, our speedometer jumped past sixty. We took the curve tighter than a fat lady's sock. The row of mailboxes sent the sign through the windshield at fifty miles per, its post gonging our noggins. In the wake of all this Dave guided us home, leaning out the driver's window. Next day, he remembered nothing—not me, my sister, or the sign.

We posted up in this cabin, which reminded me of my own family's, except this one was in a wash in Arroyo Seco, instead of in Squaw Valley, and this one had no deer's head on the wall, and wasn't surrounded by pines, but instead had been hemmed in by coast oaks. Other than that it was the same. This place gave birth to four-wheelers and dirt bikes. They spit out of the back shed in zippers of noise. Todd Smonk dealt rummy, this six-foot-seven, three-hundred-pounder, our left tackle, a scotch drinker. After high school he pissed and puked away a ride at Sac State. All their lives Todd's father had drank and gambled, and card games flicked from Todd's fingers like cigarette butts. We swam in the creek and jabbed crawdads with spears of oak. Back in Salinas, before the season, we went to the gym where Todd spotted while I pressed for air. "Come on," Todd said, his face sweat-pocked and upside-down, a frown, which was actually a smile. "Push," he urged, "you can make it."

We'd planned the party for a week, the last game on this field. Our cars herded onto the track. Benches smashed themselves to pieces and burned in the aluminum garbage cans. The desiccated scoreboard flag wiggled atop an Impala that doughnutted the fifty-yard line. Things had gotten—as they say—out of control. When the janitors' ATV headlights bumped in like a gang of wild cyclopses, I dove into Randy's Toyota. On the way out Randy said, "Who's driving your car?" We found a hill overlooking the field. Stars dotted the sky, but we couldn't see them beyond the fog that topped the valley, like a lid on a pot. Even from this distance I could see my truck, spotlighted by the Sheriff. Next morning my dad's eyebrows peaked in a way only a father's can. "Out of bed, sonny boy," he said. "Time to clean up."

At K-mart I bought boots stitched from the remains of dinosaurs. They lasted what a white person's idea of a native would call many moons. Me and the boots hiked the mountains west of the Black Rock Desert, this landscape thorned and poppied, hissing with rattlers. The desert itself was alkaline, the dust silty-fine, so that it worked into everything, even your skin, and started grinding things apart. I slipped these same boots past my toes for a day trip to The Lake with Jon. Everyone says "The Lake" like that, because people who live at The Lake have money, and then there are those living in the meadows, and saying it this way makes everyone feel rich. Jon's Mercury Cougar had rust damage that spotted it like pimples. Jon didn't even live in Reno. He lived in the desert, far from any lake. That should tell you something about his skin.

The sun had sparkled over the eastern rim of the Truckee Meadows. The heat already rippled from the parking lot's asphalt. Me and Jon did the McDonald's drive-thru for breakfast burritos and coffee, both of which nearly equaled the sun's heat, literally. I mean that after those 93 million miles through space, through that electromagnetic field blocking hazardous radioactivity, and the sixty miles of our atmosphere, the temperature was around a hundred degrees. So maybe the coffee was hotter. You might think I talk a lot. But I'm like a book when I drive: everything's between the covers. So me and Jon swerved up the Truckee River gorge and the mountains had begun to yellow with autumn. The granite made me think of a dentist's office: all gray and menacing, the boulders like molars. Jon was quiet. He liked birds: birds hardly talk at all.

We pulled up at the cabin, a pre-fab sentried by pines, a pair of old skis X-ing the apex of the roof, like something on a cartoon poison bottle. Grandpa had slathered a dull green paint over the wood so that the cabin would "blend in" with the natural surroundings. It resembled a barracks. From the outside, this place could've been the staging ground for some bearded radical, someone who San Francisco had failed. Inside sat evidence of a thriving thrift store. Even the books were *Reader's Digest Condensed*, which made me think of soup. A deer's head stared over the kitchen and hallway, above the cuckoo clock and the liquor, and the windows that squinted over the California brome and, across the road, Squaw Creek rippling cold and white with ripples. The creek had once slithered with brook trout. But they built hotels upstream. Instead of trout there are tourists, which are almost the same thing.

Jon was like a cow except he was skinny. What I mean is, he never moved fast, and didn't think it was important, for example, to know that over the next hill would be either a waterhole or more cracked earth. He was Southern by the grace of his parentage. His daddy gave me 8 AM beers at their ranch-style home, browning out under the sun in Spanish Springs. His mama made me toss down plates of eggs. Old Glory crossed the Stars and Bars above their television, a most honored spot in the living room. I believe Jon had frequented monster truck exhibitions. After a first draft of this, when he read what I wrote, Jon looked at me differently, a sadness tilting his eyes, making his baldness seem balder. I always imagined that Jon wanted to feel the inside of the back of my skull with his knuckles. I swallowed another beer in two swallows. It's only now that I can look back and say what kind of an idiot I've become.

Once me, Fredo, Moses, and goons I can't remember, went to Kings Beach for the Fourth of July. That morning I had gobbled up an eighth of psilocybin and, driving in to Tahoe City, when I steered into the Safeway parking lot for beer I narrowly missed fendering a bicyclist into a drainage ditch. "Kings Beach" is accurate—the beach part anyway—for a strip of yellow pulverized boulders crescenting a tiny bay. Who or what the kings were I couldn't say. Kids—18 to 24 year-olds—speckled the sand like chocolate chips. I could've been staring at a massive cupcake-thing: the bright sun, the blue water, a billion dark bodies casting shade. Jet skis roared and spit past the buoys. When I was a child I came here with Grandpa and the highway was one lane. You pulled over and let the oncoming traffic inch around you. I'd like to say we were in Grandpa's Model A, but really (that time) he drove a Ford pickup. But then, this Fourth at The Lake—the time I'm talking about—the shore swarmed with ass and tits and money. The water was a spill of two-stroke oil. So, I watched Fredo get drunk and throw up. His vomit undulated in the sand. Whenever someone moved they left a ghost. When I swerved back to normal, around noon, I drove into Reno, and to work at The Men's Wearhouse. To my first customer that afternoon I said, "Happy Independence Day! What the hell are you doing here?"

The summer they began construction on the Resort at Squaw Creek the walls shuddered with each explosion. Grandpa said they used dynamite to fell the trees. A chopper choppered them out somewhere where I'm sure they were cut up and used to build the exact hotel they had died for. In this sense, they never left. But the creek silted up. There was no horseback riding that summer. Granny baked the fiesta casserole and it tasted the same as always.

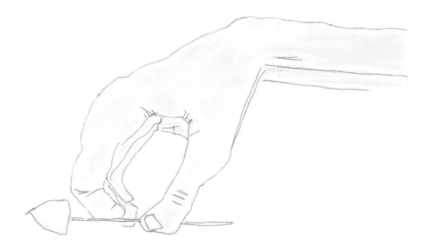

Take this mushroom and eat, for it is psychedelic, and has been broke from a quarter ounce for you.

We walked to the hotel, down Winding Creek, up Squaw Valley Road, then along Squaw Creek. We'd slung towels over our shoulders, my brother's summer-browned. The building was something the bad guys would build in a science fiction film—all tinted glass and black steel—nestled amongst pines and peaks scarped from snow. The employees' dark slacks and creamy jackets made them cop-like. The pool jutted and curved in angles, and a tiny waterfall strung into a grotto. All the other kids—those actually staying at the hotel—cheated, peeking through wrinkled lids during Marco Polo. I found a squirmy redhead in my headlock. He kicked and wailed, and all the walk home the asphalt stung our feet.

At the cabin I pawed around the shelves and end tables, scouring them for books. I eyed through all the Stephen King, with the cats and babies coming back from the dead, and cars that wouldn't ever break down. I couldn't get past the first page of anything written by this guy named Michener. I found a blue book, the title hardly legible, scrawled in gold script: *The Tales of Tahoe*. There was a Washoe Indian Chief who built fires on the concrete floors of cold offices, who ate way too many peanuts. He was a cartoon with a funny accent and handed-down white men's clothing. He said that The Lake was once a great swamp filled with quicksand. There was a polar bear and an Indian brave. There was a love story. I carried the book home, tucked into my backpack all the ride in Granny's Olds. I found a tale about raccoons, another about Big Chief. I found this version of The Lake, one that has been replaced with Taco Bell. I like the Fire Sauce.

Kanuwapi was a Washoe who scavenged other families' trash. Nights, he ran his fingers through the chief's daughter's black strands. The chief dictated: Kanuwapi had to prove his worth. Kanuwapi wandered north and found a bear like a white-painted farmhouse. Kanuwapi's arrows were mosquitoes on the bear's fur, until the Evil One whispered for Kanuwapi to shoot into the bear's nostrils. When the bear roared and chased, Kanuwapi led him south, to the mountains, to the swamp and quicksands, where the Washoe lived. The bear mired his legs with death. Storms covered him, and everything, with ice and snow. When the snow melted, where the swamp had been, there sat The Lake, and the Washoe named it "Tahoe."

My first trip to the cabin, with Grandpa, the snow caked on the power lines above I-80, the radio squelched, and we putzed forward, the tire chains rattling like metallic bones. Grandpa dug up the logs he'd split the summer before and stacked between the pines. We kept the fire glowing, but the heat swept up the chimney. We swaddled ourselves in blankets and blew rings with our breath. Uncle Dave took the prime rib to the resort at Alpine Meadows, where the generator kept the kitchen running. Dave was an old hippie. His hair ran down to his ass. His favorite word was *man*. He'd say, "Aw, man," to everything, even in place of *Peace Be With You* after the Our Father. When the chef came in to work, and found Dave in his kitchen, he said, "Get out of my kitchen, Hippie." Uncle Dave said, "Aw man, I've got to check my prime rib." The chef said, "Like hell you do."

The Truckee River leaks out of Tahoe and winds north at the crest of the Sierra. It descends east and carves into the Truckee Meadows, into Pyramid Lake, then evaporates and is reborn in clouds. Truckee-the-town is named after Truckee-the-river, which is named after Truckee-the-Washoe, a name that was not a name at all but probably Washoe for "hello". North of Truckee, half-froze in winter: Donner Lake. 1847: thirty-five starved. Grandpa said "cannibalism." My nine-year-old ears, sponge-like, soaked up the tale, on the porch overlooking the mule ears, a sunset pinking Squaw Peak, barbecued chicken blackening my fingers.

Grandpa heaved me onto the bank, yelled me toward the entrance. I pawed my way and found a shovel, then the front door. Inside, the deer's head gleamed back in the shadows. Grandpa's moustache had caked with icicles. He had flown during WWII. He had an overbite. When he died, what I noticed most were his teeth.

At the cabin, Jon pissed and I leafed the books for trails. The deer's eyes followed Jon down the hallway. Jon said, "That's a little deer your granddaddy shot. How old is this cabin?" I said, "Here's a picture of me sledding. That's my brother and sister. Here's my grandparents in their Model A." Whisky lined the cart of liquor below the tiny deer's head. I thought about a drink and thought about a drink and thought about a drink and thought about a drink.

Artifact 23: *Since estrangement is a notion referring to a plethora of phenomena according to several complex psychosocial theories (broadly construed), this "meaning" will comprise psychosocial generalizations.*

We'd gone to the cabin with our fathers, who'd enrolled us in YMCA Indian Guides. This organization's goals were in the right place, if not mixed up. Y-Indian Guides Motto: "Pals Forever"—a direct translation of a native slogan. Y-Indian Guides Aims, #5: "To love my neighbor as myself"—the natives incorporated this after they gave up their heathen ways and were again born, accepting Jesus as their Savior. After dinner, Todd Smonk's dad, Guy, said he was going to the North Shore to play. The Unwritten Y-Indian Guides Aims #7: Thou shalt gamble when within 20 miles of Nevada. Guy stumbled in 8 AM next morning. His breath was what whites' Hollywood has Indians call "firewater."

Tahoe City slid past the windows down Highway 89, along The Lake's west shore. We passed Granlibakken, and near Homewood we found the turn-off from the highway, which wound between pines and crossed a stream, white with rapids in the shade. The asphalt ended and dust clouded up behind the truck. The trail rose from the road and disappeared into the mountains. The stream went deep in a meadow, and trout wiggled after mosquitoes. The water poured from the ten-thousand-foot snowpack. Jon geared his binoculars, a camera swinging from his neck, a water bottle drooping under his hairy knuckles. I stretched and breathed deep, the wheeze of cigarette lungs stealing out of me. I had twenty-two years already. Far above us loomed waterfalls: the trail's end. I would heave like a locomotive to the tree line.

The Black Creek Canyon trail had been etched into the mountain by the gouging tires of dirt bikes. Oil hung in the atmosphere. The snowmelt charged across granite. Jon and me sucked at the air as if it was one gigantic popsicle, and we couldn't get enough of its sugar at once. The sky went green in the overhanging pine. My vision turned yellow with the soil. Below, along The Lake shore, glints of sun shot like stars off the chrome of bumpers, off the windshields.

The trail ran and the stream crazed down the slope and pushed the topsoil with it, exposing the orange and gray of the granite. We would come off the mountain in to Reno with sweat sliming our calves, dust caked to our socks. We would not reach the summit. The waterfalls eluded us. We paused in the shade of aspens and sucked deep on the bottles we'd hauled with us, tired out and waterlogged. Below, the meadow spread out like a blanket. The Lake was a mirror for the sky, the stream from a jet airliner slicing the surface. The snow flowers had inched free of the pine floor and exploded bright red at our feet.

The hike had taken us over a thousand feet vertical. My legs were custard. My shirt had sponged all my sweat, and hung heavy from my shoulders. I felt like but smelled worse than a desert. The creek ran cold and deep. We wanted to dive into the brown water and dunk our heads, but instead we drove into Nevada and to Harrah's. The diner glittered like the marquee at a cheap matinee. Our waitress had cigarette lungs, like me, and we got along. Her skin resembled the mountain granite. We ate eggs and meats at 4 PM, with Budweiser. Jon was at home. I would have to leave. Eventually, Nevada would become a memory. I would hold it in my pockets like a last chip, the remainder of winnings I'd long ago thrown back in on a bet. Now I dream about the Sierra Nevada Mountains. Sometimes I wake and I've already started to dress before I realize that I won't go skiing, that Sally still breathes soft under the covers, that outside the air hangs thick with humidity, and just South gators skim the riverbeds.

Black T-shirts heaped on the cabin's couch and the TV rumbled volcanoes. No one cared about motorcycles—choppers, as they say. The crash, a pack of dogs that had hunted the house down and taken out a measly corner, clamored outside where the air was woodfire smoke. Tuna cans—shining stars—spread across the dark driveway. The bear was the size of a VW, licking up one of those star's remnants. I lit a fire on the asphalt, a supernova. I sat alone, folding black T-shirts. The wind rattled the power lines, which ticked like a refrigerator's compressor, or a car's cooling engine. The heat and smoke were solar flares to my eyes.

It was me, Sean, Ike, and Randy in Reno for the first time. The heat emanated from the desert floor, like we stood atop an enormous range. Because Sean was like a painting of a person— all emotion, and nothing to say—Todd Smonk picked on him, saying his nipples were sausage slices pasted to his chest, and Todd called him Nate, for its alliterative qualities. Todd had the creativity of a spider. Because Sean carried this look—his eyes were so dark, like black holes, they had to absorb everything—I liked him. The whorehouse—this place named after horses, and famous for its camp—swam in liquid lit blue, the interior decorated with cheap aquariums. A waste, all that water on display in a land so much devoid of it. The hookers were taken by Sean's red hair and galactic Filipino eyes. He was the kind of guy who'd say thank you to these women. Nothing happened, except for the fish, and back outside the sun seemed much brighter, and the Earth dryer and still.

Book II:

When I Moved to Nevada

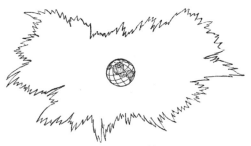

FIG. 2.— SUN-SPOT OF NOVEMBER 16th, 1882, AND EARTH.

". . . Come, my spade. There is no ancient gentlemen but gardeners, ditchers, and grave-makers: they hold up Adam's profession."

—William Shakespeare

When I moved to Nevada the Earth leaned closer to the sun and the Sierra Nevada put me closer still: everything scorched. The tree stumps were gigantic chunks of charcoal. Guitar dripped from the truck's ceiling and shot out the windows. I-80 twisted the way a river might through the Truckee's gorge. In fact the Truckee also twists in this way, and it rushed along below the cliffs. I found a post office with American flags painted all over its stamps. I became a desert rat with a signature. Afterwards came heat drizzling up from the asphalt, sun slanting through cottonwoods, arcing off the gold façade of the Reno Hilton. I met Chris Bennett when we both bought weed, and we smoked a cigarette and stared at the lenticulars—saucers that coasted in from the west.

The neighbors had chosen, special for me, a cat. They would gather me up and we would all drive to the shelter on Fifth. Their knocks pounded the door before I'd scrubbed my teeth with Crest. I lay free of headaches. I lived underground, my sole window level with the Earth's crust. Hardly any sunlight—and at night only very little casino neon—pierced my pupils. The air outside pinched my cheeks and sucked the nausea from my gut. These neighbors had slept together four or five times. They shared an apartment to save money, and because the man was from Greece. Nevada women are powerless against oily skin and stringy black hair. Leafless cottonwoods flew past us like enormous hands. My shoes squelched, soaked. At the shelter the neighbors said, "Let's see if you choose the cat we found for you." I zigged through a maze of cages. The tight, warm air swam with the smell of Windex. They chanted: did you find him? This would be the cat I named "Jules," for he was solid black and bad, my bad motherfucker. And I found this universe far from empty, baby-swaddled in a blanket woven from a billion meows.

Bob and Chris Henning and me, we drove into the desert to spotlight coyotes and jackbunnies. I bounced along in the truck's extra cab drinking Budweiser like I'd just come in from a desert haul, but it was the other way around. When the rabbits crossed into the path of our spotlight—this thing like a million candles, a miniature sun—some would stop, their little mouths nibbling something, their eyes glowing red. We popped them off with the twelve-gauge, the 9 MM, and Bob's .357 Maximum, a bazooka. When it fired, a tiny Hiroshima cauliflowered in the air and its target disintegrated. Bob laughed and said, "I love killing shit." We picked up a pair of distant glowing eyes, a coyote. Bob and Chris fired away, but before we reached the spot we had bowled the tires over a billion sagebrush clumps. When we stopped, the hiss was like a snake's with endless lungs. This was funny because a hippie at Burning Man once told Chris Henning, a Nevada native, not to park his truck on top of the sagebrush. Chris said, "Fuck you, Hippie." He'd lived in this desert his whole goddamn life and he knew that he wouldn't goddamn hurt the goddamn sagebrush. I said, "Gun it." We lost Bob when we bumped into a wash. He seemed to jump out of the bed without legs, a beachball that had sprouted a head and arms. We fell to walking two miles from the highway. Before leaving, under the truck seats, we found a flask half-full of year-old tequila that made me puke up some of my Budweiser. The Milky Way made a beach in the middle of the sea of the sky. The coyotes yipped around us, a chorus. It was so dark we could've been walking in nothing, back in the womb. When the cop said, "You boys been drinking?" Bob and Chris both said no. But me, I was slow and said, "A little."

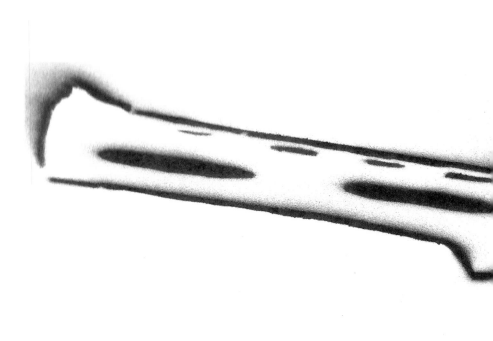

This exhibit has been marked for identification as State's Exhibit 1.

Motion to admit the .357 Maximum into evidence as State's Exhibit 1.

Bob and me kicked up road dust outside
Bridgeport when the rattlesnake, its rattles still,
nudged up against our ridged rubber tires, its
pits sensing no heat, and Bob saying, "That's a
big son of a bitch."

What's inside a rattlesnake: field mice, lightning
strikes of blood vessels, an endless dark tunnel,
a tiny muscle pumping blood cells, even when
the blood's emptied out the neckhole. At the
bottom a tiny knob waits for the next molting,
an endless rattle of rattles straining to be born.

The iceblue sky, the hill sage, the yellow
rattlesnake.

We'd got too drunk to fish off muddy banks,
the creek trout swooping for baitballs, and so
on the crossing road slithered the rattlesnake.

The rattlesnake belly sculpted dust while the
snowmelt ran silver in a mossy wash, and the
jumping trout green laced with rainbow.

The needles in our friend Timmy's arms were
the fangs of a rattlesnake.

That night, a case of beer down, the empty cans splayed around the campfire built from fallen aspens, and warming in its glow: the rattlesnake.

The silver-scarped piney crags are the west and so is a rattlesnake. And cows. Cows and coons and rattlesnakes.

Yellow as a rattlesnake eye or scale, my jaundiced skin, my belly, Bob's fingernails, our nightmares full of bears. Timmy's night visions of blue skies turned yellow as a rattlesnake belly, and he went to San Francisco where everything is white with fog, and there are no rattlesnakes.

The end of the rattlesnake: its tail, and the end of the tale: its dénouement, and the end is the end, but not for rattlesnakes.

And of rattlesnakes we can say this: they were not in biblical gardens, they have never tempted water, they are of the west, without limbs, without a sense of each skin, shed and cast away, without water, without gardens.

Brian and Jen got married at the Gold Hill Hotel in Virginia City. Everywhere, tiny white flowers like snow. But it was July and snow only pooled in shade patches on northern slopes. Brian and Jen had never even dated. They were people who'd meet—bobcats in the grasses of an alpine meadow—and snarl and fuck until Jen got pregnant. She was almost exactly like a cat, except that she was a human. Otherwise, her eyes squinted with indifference. One time she scratched up my neck in a bar bathroom.

After the wedding we tied one on. Cara kept muttering that Brian didn't know what he was doing. Cara was like that: skinny as carousel pony poles, chain-smoking Marlboro Lights. Jen would later cruise through Washoe Valley after leaving the Bar M Bar, the whisky fumes exhaust leaking out her throat. The wind and snow drove across the lake and into the cattle gathered like a bruise on the pasture. The baby girl sat uncrying as the sheriff searched and uncovered the oxycontin stash in the glove box. Meantime the mountains of the Carson Range stood against the sky, and Virginia City graced the valley's opposite summit, though long ago it had been sucked dry of silver.

We'd driven to the top of the ridge, where the casinos were stars in the desert night. The smell of Greece permeated the truck cab's air, something like old, unwashed blankets, and my friend, a Ph.D, who was from Greece. Talk of Nietzsche flooded my ears beyond where Hendrix's guitar had screeched. I didn't understand the shooting stars as free spirits, go figure. They were more like asteroids soon to be gaseous, or, for the bigger ones, meteorites. There was nothing in the way of metaphor about me. Then the sun tripped over the mountains like a clumsy fat guy. Ants followed one another over the rocks. We sucked up deep, cool breaths. For a minute they seemed like our last. But, go figure, they weren't.

Freddy had once owned a different place on the far north end of Virginia Street, near a ridge where I sometimes parked to watch the sunrise. That bar, the older one, Freddy had aptly named Freddy's. Some slut once blew Chris Bennett in the parking lot there. But this bar, the one Jess and me took over, was called The Jazz Club. It will not surprise you that jazz was never once played there—not even over the stereo.

Freddy's teeth were candy corns bitten in half and shoved into his gums. He inhaled meth the way me and Jess drank, which means that Freddy took it whenever he wasn't working, except that he tittered into the back room every hour and came out ten minutes later with his jaw grinding an invisible cud. Freddy flirted—badly, he was so desperate—with some El Dorado cocktail waitress. It had gotten late enough that for me and Jess clocks became whirlpools, washing machines on spin. We'd only just unleashed ten bucks for the fresh Cape Cods chilling our fingers, when Freddy decided he'd try to get some. Jess had one eye open and his cap brim cocked to the side. But Jess, a Portuguese skater from Oregon, always looked like that. He said we'd finish our drinks first.

When Freddy walked the woman out to the limo he'd called for her, Jess turned the deadbolt and we found the other side of the bar: a trove of shining bottles. We could've been two fat guys who'd fallen into a vat of bacon. Freddy pounded the window and screamed. We licked up the last of the whiskys we'd poured out and let him back in. His arms waved like a blonde's hair while he called the cops.

We shuffled down Fourth Street in search of the next place still open. The police never would've made it to the Jazz Club because they had corralled in front of another bar along with their fire truck and ambulance cousins. The city pulsed with their strobes. When we passed we stepped over a thin dark trickle in the gutter. The stream ran up a short driveway and into the alley. It ran into the side of the man who'd been stabbed. He lay on his side, his breathing like a puppy's. People stood around passing cigarettes, but no one seemed to notice the guy. Jess and me agreed: get the hell out of there. But instead we knelt, our palms against the man's shoulders. "Don't worry," we said. "You're going to be just fine."

Once, down above the junk, this feeling like I was part of something. Bob had wrapped his T-shirt round his head in a turban and twirled like a galaxy to the punk rock, the bulges of his stomach and droplets of sweat spinning off like planets and stars shot out of orbit, and his gas like, well, gas. My cigarette mingled with a million others. It was a protest for cigarettes. They'd gathered to say, here we are, now deal with us. Sharon's anger shot back at me for reasons I couldn't fathom, as usual. She had eyes like a cat's. Even when happy she appeared non-committal, or pissed. This million people danced with their cigarettes, without angry girlfriends. Everyone got out of Bob's way, so he might spin uninhibited. There have been one or two times since when I felt almost the same way. That bar—the Summit Saloon, way out in the dark on Fourth Street—closed. Afterwards they put up condos. That's the way it always is.

—*I love killing shit.*

The bay in the lake in the mountains gleamed emerald and our skin glistened from its water. The cliffs rose out of The Lake like skyscrapers from a boulevard. They were bald as boxers, the cliffs. I mean boxers, as in fighters. I'm just saying that it seems these days that all boxers shave their heads, and the cliffs were like that—treeless. I had dived in from a rock that stuck out from the beach like an exploding zit, forgetting my wallet folded up in my pocket. Now, as we drove away, with the green bay growing into its own tiny lake in the rearview, my driver's license had oozed and bled and I couldn't make out my own picture, nor my name, birth date, the color of my eyes, thankfully my weight—none of it—all gone.

Mike rode next to me. We passed a housing construction site covered up in blue tarp against the rain. Mike said, "In the construction community we call that a tarp." He was full of redundancies and our girlfriends' eyes rolled in the back seat. Some asshole in a jacked-up four-wheeler jumped all over my ass. I could tell that he himself was the kind of guy who'd say "jacked up," with all seriousness. Oakley Gators wrapped around his eyes.

I said, "I'm going to brake-check this jacked-up truck."

The girls' mouths drew Os in the air.

Mike said, "You girls chill. We're gonna kick some ass."

I worked with this kid named Zach who swore he never tweeked, but his teeth were being ground to nubs. This was too bad. He had a movie star's mouth, and an underwear model's hair. He lived in the basement apartment of an old brick building on Second Street. The apartment was flood damaged that New Year when the Truckee splashed over its banks. Only studs held up the ceiling. No drywall. Zach and his roommates hung blankets to mark off rooms. Everyone in that apartment worked at a bar or restaurant, so no one used the kitchen, except as a trash ground. A mound of decaying fast food and its wrapping—a tiny landfill—covered the linoleum. Flies buzzed in through the kitchen's open window and maggots wriggled in the sink.

Ten years later Mike and Jasmine took up a place in this same building, but on the top floor. Their apartment—although complete with drywall—wasn't in much better shape. I never again saw that basement and haven't a clue what happened to Zach. But when we found the apartment adjacent to Mike's unlocked and vacant, it became the site for the New Year party. At the Dollar Store we found decorations—streamers and crepe, balloons, a tiny fold-up poker table with plastic chips. We took turns in Mike's apartment snorting stuff.

By the end Dustin had pissed in the bedroom closet and the toilet had overfilled with cigarettes and tissue. The fireworks had burnt holes into the kitchen cupboards and melted the floor. A bottle rocket flew right through Bean's skirt. Dustin broke out the window with the empty keg. I woke on Chris Bennett's couch and the snow that had melted on New Year's Eve had frozen to ice. Everything in the past feels like that: slippery and cold.

Little Nickie bit off part of Mike's ear at the El Cortez Lounge. This was before the El Cortez replaced its carpets, before Mike met his girlfriend, before Nickie had her baby. The homeless would slump in and order PBRs with quarters and dimes. Polynesian tribal tattoos squiggled their way over the bartender's face, which belonged to a blond dyke. Mike had flipped Nickie's skirt and when she hollered at him he said, "You know you like it." It looked like a kiss, a love bite. I thought, that bastard's going to score after that shit he pulled. Then the blood dripped down his neck, over his fingers. We called Little Nickie "Tyson" after that.

I'd watched that fight—the Tyson one—on a big screen at the Hilton's sports book. Me and Terrence wore porkpies, chewed the ends of cigars. We'd paid fifteen bucks to watch these guys pummel each other, and it wasn't even live action. The whole thing lasted three nanoseconds. In that moment the initial quarks that cooled and lumped together to form protons and neutrons at the beginning of time, that smashed together into atoms which grouped up to make that part of Mike's ear, were again separated. A million fists flew up and voices clamored. Teaser tickets, ripped, floated down. We marched out of there and probably got drunk.

I realize that it wasn't Mike's ear—my Mike, the one little Nickie chewed up—that Tyson spit out on the mat. Then again, we did nickname Little Nickie "Tyson." So, if I want to remember it that way—that Mike was in the ring in those baggy shorts, his glove bloodied from his tattered ear—in a sense it's not far from the truth.

Figure 2.1.2: *The cochlea of the inner ear propagates these mechanical signals as waves in fluid and membranes*

She had a boyfriend but I drove her home. Still, I stopped at the man's house for weed first. Dust grew like hair on the drawn drapes and the living room was dark as a movie theater. Only the snake's terrarium on the otherwise empty bookshelf glowed with fluorescence like an exit sign. She wanted to hold the snake. I think the girl's name was Dana. She loved them, she said—snakes, that is. Though this python thing bit her—leaving a crescent of darkening maroon over the meaty part of her palm— afterwards we still puttered over Donner Pass. The boulders and pines flew by like molars and canines. We sang Aretha Franklin: "What you want, baby I got it." She had a boyfriend, I know. They always do.

I found my leather jacket at Savers, the Thrift Department Store. Me and Jake were two-thirds of a fifth of Beam down. Jake's real name was Justin. My roommate Jason we called Daryll, Terrence was Clint, Kostas we called Gus. They called me Larry. I suppose this was funny. Me and Jake rode home in a shopping cart and on a bicycle. I looped the lock and chain through the cart's wire mesh and told Jake to get in. We were clowns peddling down Oddie, falling every fifteen feet. We tacoed the bike's wheels. We turned the skin of our palms and elbows to sloppy joe mix. Back at my apartment we downed the whisky. Jake was missing teeth and grabbed his balls a lot. Once he told me a story about some hookers and crystal meth and how it was three days going before he remembered work, but he'd already been fired. He'd been working as a butcher and me and Daryll joked about how Jake would bring home the meat. This was all many years ago. Now my girlfriend and I share fifty-dollar bottles of cabernet over steaks. The leather jacket cost twenty-five bucks. I still wear it. If Sally ever wants to know where I got it, she can read this.

The snow sifted down Halloween night. The cars in the lot below became frosted cakes. We had booted a hackeysack all summer and into the fall. But now Karen and Nicole slid and stumbled, and our hands and cheeks tinged like ripe strawberries. My baseball cap's G—for Gangsta, so I thought of myself then—disappeared under the white. The trees hung and leaned like in a Dr. Seuss book. The river's gurgles interrupted our shrieks. The trick-or-treating ghosts wore ghostly powder on their ghostly sheets. Back inside, the lights buzzed a constant whir of industry. The pipes clamored and panged with Morse code. Our strawberry cheeks blossomed into cherries. Me and Nicole kneeled up to the window. I had been sliding her way for centuries and swam in a nebulous cloud of Marlboro Lights and Channel No. 5. The casinos painted Peavine Mountain neon pink. We inched closer together like Catholics. Like Catholics, all we ever did was pray.

Along the Yuba at Emigrant Gap, the campfire tossed dancing light on the pine needles, on the canyon walls. The black water curdled below. My roommate decided to grow obese. "Like Elvis," he said, "only bigger." Away from the fire the stars glittered out against the fabric of space and diamond-studded the tiny pools of snowmelt in the treeless granite. My roommate—insisting he be called Smoky, for his marijuana habit—lit a joint and jabbered about peanut butter and banana sandwiches. He would quit Reno Concrete and lounge in bed all day. I would construct a constant supply of peanut-butter-and-banana sandwiches, loaded onto a skateboard that wheeled into his room mornings, rolled out and wheeled back, evenings after my Pub shift. Abandoning our shoes and socks on the cliff, we drifted into space, chill air rushing against our eardrums, our noses pinched against the immersion—the plash and shock of glacial cold enveloping us as our breath escaped like gases from ocean-bottom vents. We pedaled for the surface and shivered on the riverbank. "I'd lie in bed and grow to over a thousand pounds," Smoke said. "Wouldn't that be amazing?" Nothing but peanut-butter-and-banana sandwiches. Then we clambered skyward, into the stars, to the warming whisky and fire.

Her skin was the color of pumpkin pie. Her lips were bumpers on her face and when we collided I didn't feel a thing. She wore a red sundress spotted with yellow and green flowers to a party full of fraternity brothers and girls in jeans and high heels. The dress itself was Latin, literally. Later, when I peeled it from her skin, the tag read *Hecho en Mexico*. At the party she flirted with Schaefer, a guy with cheeks so thick and squared they seemed full of cotton. If you punched him, he would explode. Not just his face, but all of him. Cotton everywhere. Afterwards, we drove to the ridge—this place, silent, like a peak in Darién—where I liked to watch the sunrise. "I don't want you to think I only want sex," I said. She had me unbuttoned and clambered all over my lap. She nibbled my ear, whispered, "Aye *Papi*. Why would I think a thing like that?" Trumpets might've played somewhere in the background, but probably not.

We'd closed the Pub and the orange streetlights transformed everything into this dusky Martian surface. Nick was a reed in a breeze. We'd been drinking only beer, but whenever Nick had ten dollars he took the bar to it until his barstool kept trying to walk away from under his ass, conspiring for a hard rendezvous with the concrete flooring. Some guys we didn't know brawled in the street, squared against each other, circled, a human Stonehenge. Their girls stood by, fists pounding air as they chanted no no no no no no no. Me and Timmy decided these guys could not fight in front of our bar, on our street. This sense of ownership overcomes only the most deluded and young and white, which constituted us. But I explained everything, my palms like pale twin stop signs. These fighting guys understood and started to break it up. But Nick Bender. Fucking Bender. After everyone cooled off and me and Timmy walked away, satisfied with our community duty done, Nick still stooped there mouthing "bitch" and "cock whore." Then he was on the ground, black blood running from his broken teeth. When me and Timmy ran back, bottles breaking musically and rhythmic, the girls screamed and the wind died. A neighbor cocked a shotgun. I've had better nights.

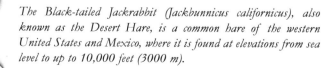

The Black-tailed Jackrabbit (Jackbunnicus californicus), also known as the Desert Hare, is a common hare of the western United States and Mexico, where it is found at elevations from sea level to up to 10,000 feet (3000 m).

75

I had this broken leg that kept me in bed, pans clamoring in my head, and the leg feeling as if someone had twisted it out of the socket then reset it, which was in fact what had happened. I couldn't drag myself downstairs nor slide behind the wheel to find a pharmacy that would fill my pain prescription. Also, a film of old Jaeger coated the inside of my mouth, and judging from the way the ceiling circled over me, driving was out of the question anyway, sans broken leg. The sun filtered through the slats covering the south-facing windows, through which I could just glimpse the mountains screaming at me.

I called the Pub and made Tyler walk to Niles' house. Niles was a painter—the kind that does buildings, not landscapes or portraits or weird abstract things, you understand. He kept a fishing tackle box locked in his dingy apartment. This place never saw daylight unless the door swung open on a squinting Niles. It was too dark even for the cockroaches. They oozed all over the garbage can outside. The cubbies of the tackle box Niles had filled with drugs: coke, amphetamines, ketamine, mescaline. Niles would say, "What kind of party tonight?" and close his eyes to pick. He carried an array of pain killers. Perhaps because of this, Niles at forty-two looked over sixty.

Once, this lady had contracted with him to run his brush over her trailer out in Sun Valley. She was beyond fat. She was an enormous mound of clothing in which a human had hid, and found a place to poke out her head. She lived with nine million cats. She'd paid, ahead of time, cash, the full amount. Then Niles never heard from her. He called, his nasal wheeze trailing off on the answering machine, but no return. You might think Niles would say fuck the job and keep the money, but he wasn't like that. He was the kind of guy who, if you showed up at his place to get help pulling your truck out of a volcano and he was all hopped up on crack, would say "First smoke this. Now we'll need a heavy-duty chain." So Niles drove to the fat cat lady's trailer and pounded the door, walked around. There was this awful smell, like at the dump outside Fernley. So Niles kicked in the flimsy door and the woman lay next to her recliner, the television droning on some hospital soap. The cats, furry vultures, had taken chunks out of her. Scratch that line about the dump; it smelled worse.

So. Tyler got the pills and drove them over. They came with instructions from Niles: "If you want to float, take these. But if you want to fly . . ."

Me and Sharon were driving into Dog Valley where Crystal Peak peaks from the myriad peaks of the Sierra. Crystal Peak is named that because the mountain is quartz and along the dirt roads through the meadows you can find perfect little geometric crystals, and because it was a peak. Why the valley's named after a dog I could never tell. Who knows what I'd said? It didn't matter. At the Pub we both poured beers and stacked up sandwiches. After our shifts we drank and sometimes sucked down joints on the back deck. When we walked in mornings we counted out one hundred twenty steps from front door to bar. We always forgot to count the steps home, but I'm guessing it took more, maybe one thirty-seven. So, when Sharon punched the windshield and it splintered into spider web, I said "Get out." She went for the beer, which we'd columned under ice in the Styrofoam cooler we'd purchased at Raley's. The cooler tore into tiny flakes that floated through the air like snow. The Pabst rolled into the ravine. I followed in the truck as she stomped off into the desert. She studied geology, rock fracture mechanics in exotic environments. She knew things about what happened to cosmic surfaces upon meteor impact. Sharon screamed "you fucking son of a bitch" and "what the fucking fuck." Her hair was like a bird's nest, a pretty brown, and just as tangled. I taunted her like an animal, which of course both of us were—*are*, if she's still alive. "You'd better get in the car or I'll leave. I'll strand you out here." She kept hollering, so I drove off, back to Reno, twenty miles. When next I saw her, at the Pub, we were drunk and we kissed. I've had a few kisses just as good, but none, I don't think, that were better.

My friend had gotten engaged, so everyone was drunk. Me and this friend were about the same size, which means we were like two adolescent grizzlies. He'd played rugby and once did so with his drawers full of an accident. Everyone called him Chafe. We decided, me and Chafe, that it was a good idea to see who could toss who off the balcony. Winter had made ice that was hard and slick as a mountain road grow over the balcony. The mountains, too, were covered with snow, and our breaths puffed as if we smoked, though both of us were thinking of quitting.

Chafe won the toss and I had broken a leg. I kept falling every few feet when I walked. Chafe tossed me again, this time into a pickup's bed, which took me to the hospital. Inside I cried for morphine because I craved the high; I was too drunk to feel any pain. The doctor said, "You're so wasted, I'm not giving you shit."

After they splinted me and crutched me, we slipped out to Knuckleheads and met the rest of our friends. There we all continued drinking, since Chafe was getting married. . . .

It had already been a night with kegs tossed through two kitchen windows before Brian broke out the coke. By then the sky had smeared pink and the snow, too. Mike lay on the carpet fingering Chris Bennett's porno, *The Bi Who Loved Me*. Tendrils from the philodendron covered the African woman carved out of the Zambezi teak. We crawled into the Jeep with a pitcher of sangria. The rails ran up the CD case and the CD itself tore through our air as we pummeled the desert. When we reached Peavine, the sky was stark and white as the snow patches beneath the sagebrush, as the drugs. It became a must for me to top Dog Valley Road.

Bob jiggled in the passenger's seat. His belly flopped around, and his beer lost its carbonation. We climbed to the summit and the snow deepened. It felt like I'd driven into quicksand. The difference was that it was snow, slippery and cold, and we weren't anywhere tropical, which is where I imagine one finds quicksand. We slid around and I strained to avoid the drop into the ravine. At the summit for a second I thought, why not? We'll go down into the valley where no one lives except deer and fox. Snow covered the dirt road a foot thick. The meadow was a blank page. Bob's eyes were like a rat's: shiny and black and smiling. "We going?" he said.

"Do it, you pussy," Mike and Chris barked. They were guys who would tuck their junk in order to look like women, even if no one had a camera.

I cradled the booze and it ran down my beard like I'd been punched.

I turned the Jeep around. Bob shook his head. "You pussy," he muttered. We could've gotten stuck and we'd all have to eat each other to survive, which would have been interesting. We'd have exchanged pinky toes first, then the next little piggy, and the next. . . .

We'd camped on Peavine in a rare pine grove. Sagebrush peppers Peavine and from its peak you can see into California, it's so clear. All night Wayne kept burning his fingers trying to pry his stew can from the embers. The stars made a planetarium show, though this was real. I kept fingering my cheeks to make sure they hadn't melted away, because they felt like that: all gooey. I said that everyone had better watch it, that they had our social security and credit card numbers, everything. Don't give anything up to them, I said. I swigged the Evan Williams. Before I explained who "they" were, I decided to make out with a boulder lining the fire pit. I was hot for it, Wayne said, the way I dove in, as one does into an emerald pool. The next morning the sun scooped into my eyeballs as if they were mounds of ice cream. The ride home I kept wondering what I was doing there.

When I moved from Nevada: Moses and Fredo stacked boxes of books in the U-haul, cussing at the sage-filled lot adjacent the building. Jules lurched around the emptying apartment as hiding places—i.e. under the bed—dismantled and walked out the door. I shattered the kitchen chairs by tossing them from the balcony. Mike, Bob, Chris Bennett—everyone—drooped their asses over barstools. When I said goodbye they turned partway and shrugged. I could have wept like a wife in this divorce (fact is, I did, manly self-denial). A sunset pinked over Crystal Peak and Peavine. Pulling the U-haul, the Jeep dragged like a poem: this way and that up the Sierra. Donner Lake and Pass were snowless and tame. From the back seat Jules wailed a fury like something from a novel.

At the Little Waldorf, which everyone called the Wall, boars' heads snouted from the knotty pine and bad punk bands spit at the college crowds. I'd wanted my five dollars back and the bass player said, "open your mouth." Before he could wad the bill in, I'd balled his collar in my fist and felt a cheek squish against my knuckles. Then someone yelled Bender's name and Jason was routing a guy who had a shaved head. Jason's arms worked like twin sets of a steam locomotive's main rods. Larry soared over the gathering bouncers and his cast-encrusted hand rebroke on Baldy's head, and sent him to the sticky concrete. On the way out, on Sierra Street, when the cops asked if we'd seen a fight, we accurately described those we imagined to be involved.

Years later, after Jason's funeral, we'd remember that night. What a scrapper he was. The time we fought at Chewi and Jug's and Jason lost his glasses. Next day, he slumped in to the bar after the glasses and found FAGGOT etched backwards on the lens, so he'd always read it, for the rest of his life.

I like to imagine that when the head-on happened, Jason was happily drunk in the passenger seat, and Nick just swerved a bit, the headlights coming like coyote eyes at the other end of a flashlight. Last, when the cars met, it was like being punched: for a second everything bright, bright white. Then black. Then nothing.

Book III:

When I Moved to Atlanta

"Then you start digging and the deeper you go, the more there is."

—John Mellencamp

We let the cat out at Meteor Crater. I leashed him to me, but he squirmed until he hooked himself under the truck and the collar turned his head into a pinched sausage. When I plucked him out, his claws ripped a canyon in my palm, so we never saw what a massive hunk of rock could do to a yet more massive hunk of rock. That night we left Jules, the cat, in the Amarillo hotel, where he squiggled under the bedsheets. Amarillo was empty silos and yards full of things that looked like Holsteins, and sometimes actual cows. Other than a one-time trip to the Sierras, and to Reno, Sean had never left Monterey Bay. He was like a kid in a Dickens novel, all pluck and smiles, squeezable cheeks. He wouldn't talk about sex or drink or his bearded father who had never learned my name. Sean wanted to go to Hooters because, like most places, he'd never been. I said the chicken wings were okay. That's what we had, the skin dripping off them like it does from the humans in nuclear holocaust films. The sauce ran into the cut on my palm and I held it out to Sean. "Don't be afraid," I said, "touch it."

In Georgia: flying cockroaches that locals call "palmetto bugs," but I know what they are. Their antennae whisp out to two and a half feet long, the driving whips to horseless carriages. And when they scurry across the deck, they do so in the way of a chocolate retriever that has just heard "walk" and "park" as he bumbles upon picnic guests. I have spied these vermin nibbling the remains of apples tossed down the descending escalators and into the subterranean stations. One told me he was a reporter with the <u>Atlanta Journal-Constitution</u>. Another, seemingly mid-fit, had lost his job as a haberdasher. He hoped something else would come along. I inched around his many prickled legs where he crouched at a street corner, the six alternating outstretched and undulating plastic drink cups rattling their dimes, tears coursing down his mandibles, a solitary violin wailing from somewhere.

When I moved to Atlanta, thunderstorms crashed across afternoons. I'd tell my homeboys in Nevada that I'd moved to this tropical rainforest. Herds of mosquitoes grazed the alleyways—mosquito-sized vampires—and heaved hordes of citizens above skyscrapers, then dropped the husks of their bodies to Peachtree Street. The hulls of destroyed brick rows lurked underground, and above, fiberglass rocketed into the rain. Hardwood floors lined my apartment, and cockroaches scrawled notes across my chest. With the humidity, I inhabited the inside of a mouth, the space between ass cheeks. Jules wailed to go outside, forever and ever.

Aedes aegypti: Whenever significant heavy rainfall arrives, greater mosquito activity is anticipated.

Oklahoma marks the South's beginning, and I knew this by the Waffle Houses: blades of grass, so I couldn't toss a mountain without hitting one. Finally, a thousand miles of asphalt already turned under our vulcanized tires, in Atlanta, Sean and I slid onto its counter stools. Only later, after having lived in the South for a minute, would I learn that the black Waffle House sat in the dark off the southbound side. Although Waffle House rules state that they do not discriminate, every Southern freeway off-ramp has two: one for black folks, one for white. The steaks in the black Waffle House were less greasy and their chili tasted like chili. This Waffle House—the white one—had an atmosphere of dense cigarette smoke. Its wrinkled and yellowed inhabitants called us Hon, like something from a sitcom. The fried eggs slid bright white out of the skillet. So, too, slid the blackened steaks. I went to the black Waffle House later, with Mark and Kimberly. Kimberly is Korean.

Atlanta apartment hunting toured me through strange-sounding byways: Cheshire Bridge, Bells Ferry, Moore's Mill Road. Everything sounded old, just as it was—antebellum, and cotton mill-studded. Finally a studio on Monroe—familiar, though still a forgotten President—emerged from the *Creative Loafing*. The landlord's voice was Southern-gay—all drawl and lilt. His eyes were shaped like rail-flattened pennies, and just as brown, like a mouse's fur. He was equally opportunistic and uncaring about the humans who pawed around his buildings. The apartment was swathed in pecan trees, and pools of standing water gurgled with mosquito larvae, their little wormy bodies waving at me. The room was cave-like, for all the shade the pecans tossed, and the lack of windows. For six years I hermitized myself in there, until I met Sally, and we moved into a place filled with light. When it came time to leave, Wayne, the landlord, said I could have extra time to pack and clean. He returned my deposit in full, minus these extra days.

My first bar in Atlanta was this underground place that had an entrance like walking down a snake's throat. I passed broken streetlamps, the glass jutting out like fangs, then, at the bottom of the darkened stair, I found the bouncer and the other victims. The bar was held together with tarp and duct tape. Everyone sported skulls that flew back with the glasses tossed down. Behind the bar, on a platform, danced the last women anyone would want to see naked. It was the stripper entourage of the senior citizen wing of the Betty Ford clinic. These women *wanted* you to touch them. They'd been objects so long, only human fingers reminded them that they had skin, and that once it did not look and feel exactly like a brown paper bag. One woman, known the world over for her poetry and television appearances and, especially, for smashing beer cans with her tits, claimed to know me. "I just moved here," I said. "Oh no, baby," this monster cooed, "I *know* you."

Eliot and I elbowed up at the Highlander, wood-paneled dark, the bar mirror stickered with Johnny Cash. The chili-smothered tot steam rubbed its yellow back against my nose. In the military, Eliot had learned that blood makes the grass grow green, so afterwards he wandered to Nevada, where everything's brown. But then he went to Georgia where all it ever did was rain. At the Highlander, sometimes the cocaine came with actual cocaine crushed up into it. The nights were a swirl of tattoos, and I had to squint to find actual people. Eliot, too, was like this: covered with text. Aptly, his poet-father had named him for the guy whose Michelangelo-talking women came and went. Once we had a morning full of PBR and Jaeger, after which I snored for two days and the world still wobbled. Eliot nursed his bald spot, moved back to Nevada, where I married him. That is, I presided over his wedding. When he left I slurred through 184 days at the Highlander and gained thirty pounds.

Travis set me up on a blind date with the woman I would call The Cackler. Her power was that, when drunk and laughing, hers was the voice of comets colliding, if they did so in an atmosphere of oxygen, nitrogen, and the lovely ill-fated trace elements, where organisms lived that could hear the cataclysm. At the end of each cackle she screeched *Larry*, as if I'd stolen her cookie. We ate roasted something, and didn't go out again. After a year of watching movies alone, we peeled each other's clothing like the skins off bananas. I tried to not be funny, and to not drink, but my mouth became a comedy that fed off wine—the marriage of tongue-to-booze-to-teeth-to-roof-of-mouth-to-air produced only more cackles. She floated continent-like in the tub and the water held islands of soap. "You said you'd try," she said. Her eyes were global warming ice caps. I asked for a ride home, then borrowed seven bucks.

If you ripped off Todd Smonk's knit collared shirt, you'd find another knit collared shirt in place of skin underneath. He was still tall, but had slimmed to this ogre-emu-like thing. His wingy hands carried fingers large and useless as feathers, and you could ski down his nose. He drank scotch and water, which, he claimed, was how he'd lost the weight. Pills hit the back of his throat the way beer hit mine. When he called, I was thrusting on top of a slut from the Highlander, a woman with more piercings than skin. It was like fucking the inside of a gumball machine. We went out—Todd and I—to strip clubs. I took him to the Clermont Lounge, where he spread himself all over a wrinkled woman's butt—it was Red Snapper, I believe—and the sunlight speared in whenever someone opened the door, like God peeking in and not liking what He found: Todd's giant beak agape, and rows of stark white teeth.

Mike and Jasmine drove up from Florida in the bus, a vehicle that had once shuttled rugrats from mobile homes to some rural Nevada education, and that now had its seats ripped out and replaced by a box springs and a mystery-stained mattress. The road through that July south Georgia sludged through a vast viscous soup: swamps and cotton fields steaming and smelling like chicken. Black men lined the roadsides and off-ramps, their palms elephant-skinned and upturned. After Mike and Jasmine made it to Atlanta the bus refused to turn over. A terrible whine like fucking cats emitted from under the hood. Before they could trudge their way back to Reno, Mike and I spit parts together and greased our knuckles. The mosquitoes made us swell under our sweat. Nights we sucked swill at the Highlander. One night we ended up with a gram of coke. We got too high to talk, which was good, since the next day the bus started, and they left.

I met Sandra at the Highlander, and her friends called her Nine, for the fingers she was not missing. The nub where the lost one (while a toddler, horseback riding accident) had once been attached stuck out from her palm like a nipple. This did not inhibit her pool game, as she warped the table with the speed of her shots. Her hair was blonder than corn silk, so I won't compare it to that. In the car, before she let me out, the tree shadows skimmed our faces like fingers, and her hand, soft in mine, counted out each digit. I imagined the ghost pinky, trailing across the ridges of my prints, grasping at me, and eventually letting go.

Sandra did my taxes. She had a computer in a room, and both were so covered with cat hair you'd think the cat had shaved herself, or that a bear had, or a bear-sized cat. Sandra's fingers—all nine of them—clacked away at the keyboard, and the sound made me think of chickens, which made me think of fried chicken, because we were on Atlanta's west side, a place that perpetually reeks of picnic. Sandra's mother helped, because when it came to numbers I might as well have been red-necked and bearded, which I was, and I slurred and stuttered through addition. The mother's perm turned her head into a globe, and her glasses became its equatorial island chain shimmering on the ocean of her face. I said "archipelago," pronouncing it archi-pel-EH-go, and both women's teeth floated in the holes of their mouths. I'd brought mac-n-cheese: my dinner contribution. No one had fried any chicken at all, though I kept smelling it.

I'd meant to surprise her. I peddled through Midtown, weaving around skyscrapers, their business people be-suited, legs and faces shorn smooth as a lake surface in November, but it was May, and I slapped at mosquitoes that fastened to my face—magnets after the iron in my blood. By the time I reached Sandra's— which we'd painted the color of a pumpkin— my skin had flushed, and my limbs had curled in, sweaty, and I resembled the engines for the trains that thundered by across the street. In my underwear I cooled, though I hoped to work up another sweat when Sandra keyed her way in. The air conditioner coughed and ants marched along the windowsill. When she slipped around the mesh of screen at the door, the blond bob of her ponytail shifted like something alive, quivering. I could've been half-naked and threatening, but only the former was true.

I'd turned vodka into air and had been breathing all day. Sandra kept the pace. The bartender was Raggedy Ann, if Raggedy Ann gained 200 pounds, and had a laugh exactly like a car's alarm. Sandra and I nibbled spinach. Eventually I waved away the Bloody Mary mix, but ordered extra olives. Raggedy Ann could've sworn me off vaccines and replaced them with booze. "I love you," my eyes beamed, and the bar top beneath the bottom of my glass festered with rings from other emptied glasses. "No, you don't," Sandra said. Her hand waved like a flag: nails red, sleeves blue. "Don't say that." Her eyes slit in the afternoon light. When we slithered out, the sedans and SUVs honked past us. One woman with curls exactly like snakes constricting her noggin, made a face I'm sure she makes when she smells her husband's farts. I waved.

Distribute several dollops of mousse onto towel-dried hair and blow dry two-inch sections at a time with a vent brush. Mist a one-inch section with styling spray and then wrap it tightly around a medium curling iron. Hold for a few seconds to set, release and repeat, alternating direction until all sections are curled.

After I'd been dumped—the bar top snowed in with cigarette ash turning to slush in Jameson—some cokeheads took me home. The woman's tits were bowling balls in terms of their fakeness and hardness. The guy's HIV—so they told me—made me snort with my own bill. My legs jumped and my stomach filled with lizards' feet. I'd need six more whiskys before my lids could seal shut that night. But first, I'd get a ride back to the bar in a Honda littered with pecan shells and fast food wrappers. Inside, nothing had changed: cigarette smoke swirled, and everyone inside floated, waiting for something to happen.

Sally's Toyota met me at the street and inside Sally could've been bespectacled and a Republican, but was merely bespectacled. We went for bell pepper and breadcrumbs. Our plates remained layered with meatballs and marinara. Although the conversation ran as ticker tape from the machines of our mouths, our stomachs had wadded themselves into chewing gum. Jules jumped between her and me, right when I leaned in. The rain pattered like paws on the windowsill, and we missed the Cardinals and Mets, but later learned the rain had rained them out. When it thundered the light went dim, then bright again. After Sally went home I felt a slight tug—the Highlander down the street—but I stayed rolled in my covers, awake as if I'd run my veins full of stuff that's meant to keep you that way, only I'd barely finished a glass of Chianti. It still graced the table, staining the cloth with myriad rings, light purple, and darker and darker.

Sally and I hiked Kennesaw Mountain, which, as far as mountains go, is a crumb on the table of the Earth. There isn't much to it. And if the Sierra Nevadas are loaves of bread . . . . Years ago, armies drug cannon and bodies through the pine needles and mud in these hills while Sherman was fixing to set everything ablaze. The tiny people driving their tiny cars in the tiny towns below grew tinier as we mounted the summit trail. The rocks sat bald as rocks, evidence that even before the North ravaged the South, glaciers had slithered through, eating everything and giving birth to boulders. Our sandwiches were lined with turkey we had not shot nor beheaded. Later, when we left the mountain, we did so in a Toyota made from and powered by paleobotanical goo. Sally's pants modestly covered her ankles. She hummed and sighed when I fumbled through my past: my parents were Yankees, and I came from West to East, and I'd once smoked crack. Maybe more than once. "Just to lay everything out there," I said. My fingers felt for skin to pick and instead pulled at a tree's. "I'm only half-Southern," Sally said, and she explained that only her mama came from Georgia. That made me feel better.

I bought Huey Lewis on iTunes. He was 1985. I mean, if a year could sing and play sax at the same time, this was it. Of course, Huey Lewis did not play sax, but he might have. Sally thought I should purchase a new pair of Vans, wrap my curls in a bandana. We made fajitas, which I pronounced fa-gi-tas, with a soft "g", you know, like vaginas. I hadn't any money, no fame. My credit card had disintegrated. Every day the trains slid by like snakes, their window-scales reflecting sunlight. My sweat—pooling on the platform beneath my Vans, which had torn and lipped like stupid open mouths—made an ocean, and I named my ocean Billy. In my head, my parents and I rode the station wagon up I-80, toward Donner Pass. The heater reddened our cheeks. The world was white with snow, which was what flashed by the roadside, then below the deep blue lake and, above, a page for a sky.

I spin this out—this paragraph—from this desk, while Sally's tiny feet, in their miniature sneakers, with the little swooshes, hike away this morning on her trek to the train station. Sally's lab coat's woven from bleached poly-cotton, and from work her eyes glint blue behind her glasses as she plucks bullets from the poor's limbs, and fingers closed the eyes of the dead. Sally has anchored herself here, to me now, when once she blew her breath into clouds in the Swiss winter. I am trying not to drink so much. Years ago, contractors parked the hospital, checkered with windows, across from the downtown train station, and from there the trains screech south to the airport, where everyone unloads to lift off for far-away runways. Before Sally returns this evening, when I have finished this paragraph and said to myself, good job, I will bumble storeward for chicken and veggies and begin cooking them for her, my pretty doctor. And I'll hope, like I do everyday, that she will in fact come home.

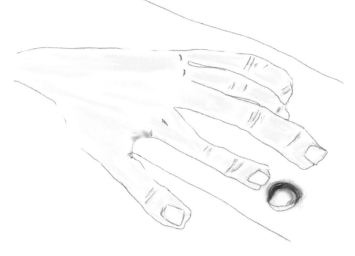

Sally had shipped a bikini, sunscreen, and herself off to Belize. Jules curled up on the bed for a minute—a real, and not a Southern minute—then he'd stretch and whine in front of his dish. Only his whiskers, bleached with age, were visible against his black fur and the black room, and they bobbed and floated as he yawned and paced. So, as anyone can understand, the bar ebbed at my gut.

When I got to the Highlander Jackson said, "Professor, Ribbon?" as he always had, and he slid the Pabst my way. This guy was the sketch of cliché, if the sketch was done in charcoal. His dreadlocks ran to his ass and his voice was like a dumptruck's engine. His belt buckle sported the Stars and Bars. He ranted that it was heritage, not hate, as he slammed Strega. He hadn't seen what Sally and I had seen: in the museum, the photos from the 60s, the little black girls caged for praying, marchers to Selma and flags waving their spit and obscenities from the road shoulder.

It was like I'd never left, etc. I became a cliché myself, once I walked in. Not the flat beer, not even the free Jaeger at my fingertips, could keep me curved over that bar.

Jamie Iredell was born in Carmel-by-the-sea, California, and grew up near Castroville. He moved to Reno, Nevada for his Bachelor's and Master's dregrees, and to Atlanta for his PhD. His writing has appeared in many magazines, among them *The Chattahoochee Review*, *The Literary Review*, *Keyhole*, *Zone 3*, *Descant*, *elimae*, *Lamination Colony*, *Elysian Fields Quarterly*, and *Weber: The Contemprary West*.

Christy Call's recent work includes cover art and illustrations for the chapbooks *Pocket Finger* and *Before I Moved to Nevada* (Publishing Genius Press 2008, 2009) and *How the Broken Lead the Blind* (Willows Wept Press 2009). She serves as the in-house artist for *Dispatch Litareview*, and has work forthcoming from Paper Hero Press and *Pank*. She is also allergic to pineapple and does not eat pineapple here: www.christycall.com.

Also from Orange Alert Press:

Most Likely You Go Your Way And I'll Go Mine
        by Ben Tanzer (August 2008)

Sunlight At Midnight, Darkness At Noon
        by Hosho McCreesh/Christopher Cunningham
        (May 2009)

LaVergne, TN USA
04 October 2009
159718LV00001B